Wild Goose Lake

First published in German under the title *Das Wasser der Wildgans*
© 1993 Verlag J F Schreiber GmbH, Postfach 285, 73703 Esslingen
English version retold by C J Moore from the Chinese folk tale
English version © 1993 Floris Books, 15 Harrison Gardens, Edinburgh
British Library CIP Data available
ISBN 0-86315-171-X   Printed in Belgium

Wild Goose Lake

A Chinese folk tale
Illustrated by Anastasia Archipova

Floris Books

Long, long ago in a distant part of China, there lived a farmer with his daughter, Water-lily. They lived in a small mountain village, working the fields on the bare mountainside. As Water-lily worked daily in the fields, she would sing the beautiful songs of the mountain folk.

One year there came a terrible drought. Many long months passed without rain. The soil in the fields dried and hardened, the crops did not flourish and the people began to go hungry. Water-lily did not sing in the fields any more.

Now the farmer and his daughter had to find ways to keep themselves. Water-lily was sent up the mountain every day to cut bamboos. She carried the heavy loads back down the mountain slopes and made them into brooms. Then she had to travel the dusty roads to sell her brooms in the markets.

One day Water-lily climbed higher than she had ever been before. On her way back with her bamboos, she discovered a blue

lake glistening under the cloudless sky. It must be the lake that she had heard of, known as Wild Goose Lake.

"Look at all that water," she said to herself. "If only I could find a way through the mountain to let some water flow to the village."

At that moment a wild goose flew past and called to her: "Water-lily, only with a golden key can you open the mountainside."

As Water-lily puzzled over the bird's message, she heard a parrot squawking in a nearby tree.

"Parrot," she asked, "where will I find the golden key to unlock the mountainside?"

"First you must find the Dragon King's daughter," replied the parrot. "Only she can help you reach the golden key."

Water-lily went on her way, as puzzled as she was before. Soon she came into a pine wood and there stood a handsome peacock.

"Peacock," she asked, "where will I find the Dragon King's daughter? Only she can help me reach the golden key and open the mountainside to let the water flow down for my people."

The peacock answered: "The Dragon King's daughter loves music. You must sit by the highest peak of the mountain and sing songs for her. Then she may come."

Water-lily went to the sit by the highest peak of the mountain and started to sing her songs. On the first day, she sang of the snowy tops of the mountains and the blue skies. But the Dragon King's daughter did not come.

On the second day, she sang of the waterfalls and the greenest grass that grew beside the brooks and streams. But the Dragon King's daughter still did not come.

On the third day, she sang of the spring flowers in the fields, and the summer crops and the autumn fruits on the trees.

Suddenly there stood the Dragon King's daughter.

"Where do you come from?" she asked Water-lily.

"My name is Water-lily," explained the girl. "I live at the foot of the mountains."

Then she told the Dragon King's daughter about the drought in the fields and the suffering of her people.

"I am looking for the golden key to open the mountainside," she said, "so that I can let some water down from the Wild Goose Lake to relieve the villagers of their hardship."

The Dragon King's daughter had a kind heart and she wished to help Water-lily, although she was afraid of her father.

"The Dragon King hides the golden key in his treasure chamber in the mountain," she told Water-lily. "A fierce eagle guards the entrance and will kill anyone who tries to set foot inside."

"How then can we reach the key?" asked Water-lily.

"I will help you to lure the eagle away with singing songs. Then you may have a chance to get inside the cave, if you are quick."

The two of them went and hid near the cave. There they sang songs until the eagle opened its eyes and started to look around. The Dragon King's daughter crept further and further away, singing as she went, until the eagle, spreading its wings, flew after the sound.

As fast as she could, Water-lily rushed into the cave, creeping through the narrow entrance. She looked all around but could not see a golden key anywhere. With her heart pounding, she searched in all corners of the cave but there was no sign of the key.

As she turned to leave in despair, in her haste she kicked over a wooden casket on the floor which spilled open, and a golden key fell to the floor.

Water-lily picked up the key and ran from the cave.

Water-lily found the Dragon King's daughter waiting for her near the cave. The two of them ran across the mountain slopes to the edge of Wild Goose Lake. There was a mysterious gateway in stone that Water-lily had not noticed before. With the golden key, Water-lily opened the stone doors and the waters of the lake started to gush out.

But the force of the gushing river was too great. As it fell to the fields below in the valley, everything was in danger of being washed away. And very soon the entire lake would flow away!

"Quick, Water-lily," called the Dragon King's daughter. "Throw your bundle of bamboo shoots into the water!"

Water-lily quickly did as she was told, and watched in amazement as the Dragon King's daughter raised her arms and started to cry out in a strange tongue. Suddenly the bamboo shoots began to grow and grow, until they stemmed the rushing flow from the open doorway of the mountain.

The bamboo shoots slowed down the water, and the broad river turned into a gentle stream which flowed peacefully down among the rocks and slopes of the mountain.

When the Dragon King found the empty casket in his treasure chamber, he angrily called his daughter to him.

She confessed to her father how she had helped Water-lily to save the villagers in the valley below.

In his rage, the Dragon King turned his daughter out of the palace.

The Dragon King's daughter went down into the valley and lived
from then on with Water-lily in their village farm. A new stream
flowed gently near their fields. They would never again suffer from
drought in the village.

And so Water-lily and the Dragon King's daughter lived
peacefully, and daily sang the songs of the mountain folk that they
both loved.